EVANSTON PUBLIC LIBRARY

W9-AOM-646

INTERIM SITE add M

JPicture Newbe.C

Newberry, Clare Turlay,
 1903-
Marshmallow /

DUE
1992

Caldecott
Honor

F

F

AU

M

MARSHMALLOW

MARSHMALLOW

Story and Pictures by

Clare Turlay Newberry

HARPER & ROW, PUBLISHERS

EVANSTON PUBLIC LIBRARY
CHILDREN'S DEPARTMENT
1703 ORRINGTON AVENUE
EVANSTON, ILLINOIS 60201

MARSHMALLOW

Copyright © 1942 by Clare Turlay Newberry

Printed in the U.S.A. All rights reserved.

Library of Congress Cataloging-in-Publication Data
Newberry, Clare Turlay, date–
    Marshmallow : story and pictures by Clare Turlay Newberry.
      p.   cm.
    Summary: A cat who is used to being the center of attention learns
to share his home with a rabbit.
    1. Rabbits—Juvenile fiction.   2. Cats—Juvenile fiction.
[1. Rabbits—Fiction.   2. Cats—Fiction.   3. Friendship—Fiction.]
I. Title.
PZ10.3.N423Mar 1990   89-20052
[E]—dc20   CIP
                                              AC
ISBN 0-06-024460-7   ISBN 0-06-024461-5 (lib. bdg.)

For

Ellen Kearns

OLIVER was a cat of middle-age, gray with tabby markings. He was a bachelor without wife or kittens, and lived in an apartment in Manhattan. A housekeeper, Miss Tilly, who had been with him since kittenhood, looked after the place and prepared his meals.

Many a cat has to catch his dinner before he can eat it, but Oliver was lucky. When he was hungry all he had to do was mention the fact to Miss Tilly, and she would open the refrigerator and get out his liver or chopped beef.

Peace and quiet was what he wanted

As Oliver never went out he did not know that the world was full of other animals. How could he, when he had never met any of them, socially or otherwise? The only mice in his life were the gray flannelette ones filled with catnip that he received at Christmas, and the nearest thing to a rabbit he had ever seen was a stuffed plush Easter bunny that had been given to Miss Tilly with a box of candy.

But Oliver did not care. Peace and quiet was what he wanted, and his meals on time.

Life, however, cannot always be like that. One day Miss Tilly called him from the kitchenette.

"Kitty, kitty," she called. "Come here, I have a surprise for you."

"Prr'owrr!" replied Oliver, and he hurried to the kitchenette, expecting to find dinner served in its usual place under the sink. But it wasn't dinner this time. Miss Tilly really did have a surprise for him.

She was smiling at something she held in her two cupped hands. It was small and white and furry.

"What do you think of this, Oliver?" she said. "Its name is Marshmallow." She held the furry thing to her cheek for a moment, as though it were very nice indeed. Then she set it on the floor.

It had tall ears, pink eyes, a wiggly nose, and twitchy whiskers. And to Oliver's dismay it was *alive*!

Oliver was appalled. He took one wild look at the creature, then squinched his eyes tight shut, as if he could not bear the sight of it.

"Oliver, what is the matter with you?" cried Miss Tilly. "Don't tell me you're afraid of a little tiny baby bunny!"

But Oliver *was* afraid. He was too frightened even to run away, but crouched in a corner of the kitchenette, opening and closing his eyes as if it actually hurt them to look at a rabbit.

As for Marshmallow, he paid no attention to anybody. He was a very unhappy little bunny. All he wanted was to be at home again with his nice warm furry mother. If he had been a

kitten he would have mewed. If he had been
a puppy he would have howled. And if he
had been a baby he would have cried his
eyes out. But being a bunny he just sat still
and felt sad.

However, he cheered up a bit when he had his dinner—a raw carrot with its green top, and a bowl of rolled oats—dry, not cooked the way people like them. The bowl said D O G on it, for the shop where Miss Tilly had bought Marshmallow did not have any dishes with R A B B I T or B U N N Y on them. But as Marshmallow could not read, this did not much matter.

He ate the green carrot-top first, for he was thirsty. Then he munched part of the carrot. After that he tried the rolled oats, eating with little quick nibbles, *crunch-*

crunch-crunch, and with his front paws in the dish. When he had finished eating, he hopped into the bowl and took a nap!

That night Marshmallow slept in the bathroom. Miss Tilly made him a bed out of a folded towel so he would be comfortable, but it was not the same as having a soft, furry mother to cuddle against. Still he did not cry.

Nor did he yowl for his breakfast the next morning.

"If only you were nice and quiet like that, Oliver," yawned Miss Tilly when Oliver woke her, as he always did, with frantic scratchings and meowings at her bedroom door. He was even earlier than usual this morning because he was so excited over having a new animal in the house.

Miss Tilly warmed some chopped beef for him, gave Marshmallow another carrot, and made herself some coffee and toast. Then she sat down at her typewriter and wrote

A POEM IN PRAISE OF RABBITS

A bunny is a quiet pet,
A bunny is the best thing yet,
A bunny never makes a sound,
A bunny's nice to have around.

Puppies whimper, bark, and growl;
Kittens mew, and tomcats yowl;
Birdies twitter, chirp, and tweet;
Moo-cows moo, and lambkins bleat;

Some creatures bellow, others bray;
Some hoot, or honk, or yap, or neigh;
Most creatures make annoying noises,
Even little girls and boyses.

A bunny, though, is never heard,
He simply never says a word.
A bunny's a delightful habit,
No home's complete without a rabbit.

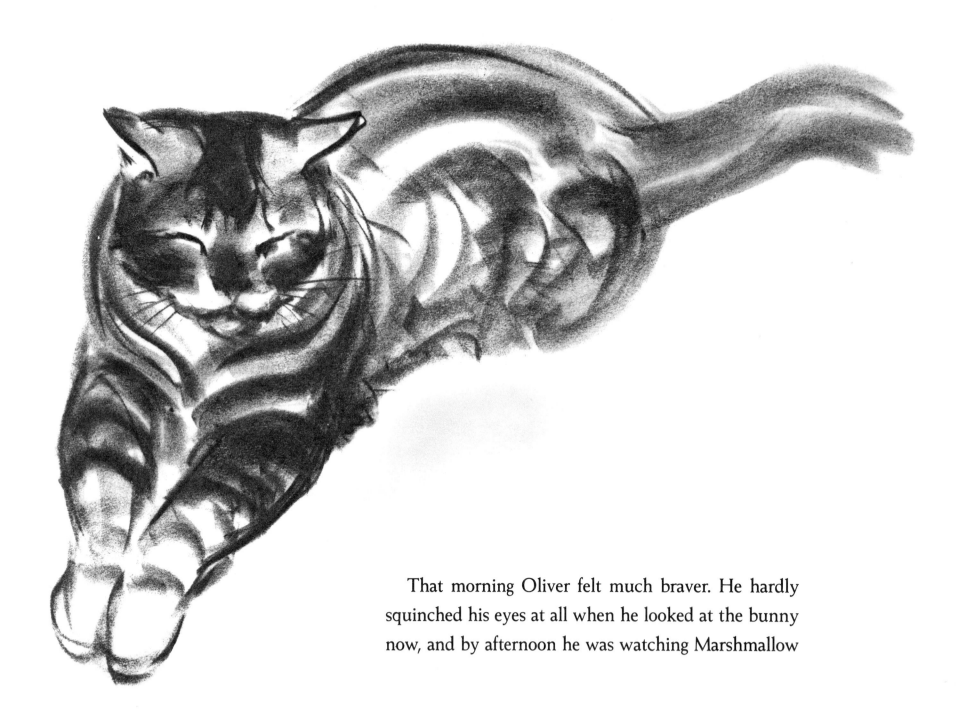

That morning Oliver felt much braver. He hardly
squinched his eyes at all when he looked at the bunny
now, and by afternoon he was watching Marshmallow

with an expression that would have frozen the blood of an older and wiser rabbit.

Marshmallow, however, was a very young rabbit, so young that he scarcely noticed what went on around him. He was like a tiny new baby that cannot yet focus its eyes. He ate when he was hungry and the rest of the time he slept, with his paws tucked up under him to keep them warm.

He certainly didn't act very dangerous, and presently Oliver grew bolder. He began creeping toward the sleeping bunny, his eyes glaring wickedly. But just as he lashed his tail and got ready to spring, Miss Tilly cried,

"Oliver! Don't you dare hurt that bunny!"

Oliver sat up, blinking innocently, as if to say, "Why, Miss Tilly, what an idea! I wouldn't dream of such a thing!"

But Miss Tilly was not so sure.

"This just isn't going to work out," she told herself sadly. "Cats always have hunted rabbits, and I suppose they always will." She put Oliver in the other room, and after that she did not let him come near Marshmallow.

Marshmallow began to notice more

Soon Marshmallow began to notice more, just as any baby does as it grows up. He went lolloping about the apartment, sniffing things, and then tasting them. And nearly everything seemed to taste pretty good.

He nibbled the rugs, working very hard in one place until he had gnawed a little bare spot before moving on. He stood on his hind legs and yanked books out of the bookcase. He chewed the chair and table legs. And every time Miss Tilly sat down for a moment he came hopping up cheerfully to untie her shoelaces. He was a very busy little bunny. Marshmallow was the only live rabbit Miss Tilly had ever known personally, and she was surprised to find that he nibbled so many things besides carrots. She wrote another poem on her typewriter, which she called

A SOLEMN WARNING
TO RABBIT LOVERS

A bunny nibbles all day long,
A bunny doesn't think it's wrong.
He nibbles mittens, mufflers, mops,
He only pauses when he hops.
He nibbles curtains, lamp-cords, shoes,
He only stops to take a snooze.

Sofa pillows, ribbons, rugs—
He takes a mouthful, then he tugs.
Galoshes, boxes, books, and string—
A bunny nibbles everything.

Whenever Miss Tilly went out, she left the two animals in separate rooms, for she did not trust Oliver. One afternoon she stayed out later than usual, and when Oliver woke from his nap there was no dinner waiting for him under the sink. He thought he'd better remind her about it, so he trotted to the door of the other room and said, "Prr'owrr!"

There was no answer, but he could hear odd sounds in the next room, small scuffling noises that caused his eyes to widen and his ears to point suddenly forward. These sounds were made by Marshmallow's little feet, as he went lippity-lippity around the room, skidding every now and then on the hardwood floor.

Marshmallow was feeling gay. He had eaten all the carrot he wanted, and quite a lot of a new magazine that Miss Tilly had carelessly left on the floor when she went out. And he had discovered her old plush Easter bunny on the sofa, and had

thoroughly nibbled its whiskers. Now he was just frolicking about the room, skidding merrily on the smooth floor and kicking up his heels for sheer joy of being alive.

On the other side of the door Oliver was listening and sniffing, and sniffing and listening, while his eyes grew bigger and bigger.

"Prr'owrr!" he said again, and scratched impatiently at the door. When this did no good, he stood up on his hind legs and patted the doorknob. Finally he reached up both forepaws, and with one on each side of the knob he worked it this way and that. At last there was a small *click*, the door swung ajar, and Oliver padded silently into the next room.

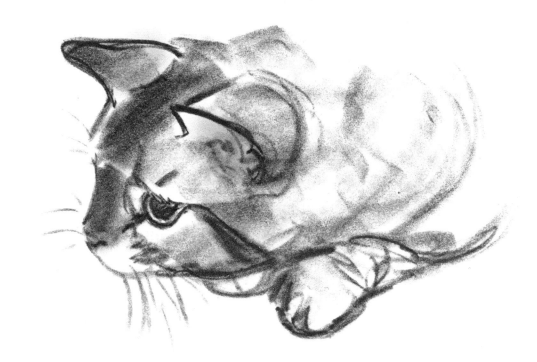

And there was that rabbit, skipping about as if he hadn't a care in the world. He didn't see Oliver come in, but went on playing a little game he had just that moment invented. He would dash several feet in one direction, stop suddenly and spring into the air. Then he would turn, dash back to his starting point, and jump again, back and forth, back and forth. It was a very gay and pretty sight.

Oliver watched it with great interest. Each time the little rabbit whisked by him he lashed his tail and got ready to spring.

But somehow he couldn't quite make up his mind to do it. Perhaps he remembered that Miss Tilly had told him not to hurt the bunny, or perhaps he was still just a bit afraid.

Suddenly Marshmallow sat up tall and stared at the cat, his soft nose twitching rapidly. He looked most inquisitive but not in the least alarmed.

What was this great striped animal, he wondered. Could it possibly be his mother in a new fur coat?

And while Oliver hesitated, trying to make up his mind to pounce, all at once

Marshmallow sat up tall

Marshmallow scampered joyfully up to him and kissed him on the nose!

Oliver flinched and drew back, aghast. Then curiosity overcame his fear, and he sniffed the bunny eagerly. Marshmallow shut his eyes and snuggled close, blissfully happy to have found another furry animal. If this were not his mother it must at least be a very near relation.

Even when Oliver opened his jaws and took hold of him with his teeth, Marshmallow was not afraid. He lay quite still, and the next moment Oliver had let go and was licking his face as tenderly as any mother cat with her kitten. And like any mother cat he licked the fur in the wrong direction, so that it stood on end and looked all mussed up. But Marshmallow did not mind, he was so happy to have a mother's care at last.

When Miss Tilly got home she found them asleep on the floor, Oliver's head resting upon Marshmallow as though he were a little white fur pillow.

After that she let them play together every day, for she saw that they were friends. They romped like two kittens, and wherever the cat went Marshmallow followed, lippity-lippity, right at his heels. And whenever Oliver lay down to take a nap,

He licked the fur in the wrong direction

The bunny cuddled up to him

the bunny cuddled up to him as close as he could get. He could scarcely have loved Oliver more if he *had* been his mother.

Oliver forgot that he had ever thought of Marshmallow as a strange animal to be pounced upon. He adopted the little bunny and brought him up as his own kitten, often scrubbing him so thoroughly that his fur stood on end for hours. And although Oliver never said so, I cannot help thinking that in time he came to agree with Miss Tilly, that

> A bunny's a delightful habit,
> No home's complete without a rabbit.

Brighten your home with a bunny,
He's fat, he's frisky, he's funny.
He's soft, he's downy,
He's cute, he's clown-y,
Oh, brighten your home with a bunny!